To Haley,
with best wishes
from

Don x

FEARLESS FRED'S
Big London Adventure

Written & illustrated by
Dorothy Lloyd Griffiths

My name is Fred. I'm called Little Fred as
I am just a puppy, six months old.

I am a Border Terrier, my coat is brownish and I have
lots of bushy whiskers round my nose and eyes.

Food gets in my whiskers when I eat but
I can clean them with my paws.

Our house is tall with lots of stairs.

We have a green front door with red flowers in pots.

I look at people going by but I don't
bark them. It might scare them.

We are very careful when we go out
as our road is very busy.

I have lots of toys to stop me being
lonely when my family go out.

I like bear and mouse but best is my big bone.

Alfie and Isla are my brother and sister
who are kind and play with me.

They take me for walks in the park so
that I can run and meet my friends.

I must tell you about my exciting adventure.

My family went out to the shops and I had to stay at home.
I had a sleep then I played with my toys, mouse and bear.

I chewed my bone then I felt very bored.

I looked round the kitchen. I found a ball of string. It seemed to get in a muddle so I left it alone.

Then I saw something which made my eyes open wide.

I could get into the garden through a "cat flap" in the kitchen door, which is odd because we don't have a cat.

It would be nice to have a cat.

Mouse and a bear would like a new friend as well.

I went into the garden and started to roll around in the grass as my back can feel a little itchy and the grass is soft and green.

I looked to see where I had buried my bone. I am only a puppy and I can't remember everything can I?

Then I found a gap in the fence.

That was very easy, I brushed some soil off my whiskers with my paws.

Now I can look for my family and it would be a Big Adventure.

I started to walk down the road.

I had to be careful as the road outside our
house is very busy with big black cars.

They are called taxis and very large red cars which are called buses.

I crossed the road on a black and white crossing which
is called a Zebra Crossing but I couldn't see any zebras!

As I trotted along everyone wanted to pat my back
but I took no notice of them and went on my way.

A lady with a big hat on thought I
was lost and tried to pick me up.

That was silly I was having an adventure
and did not WANT to be picked up.

Just in front of me was a very large bridge. I
went onto the bridge and looked at the river.

I next saw a large shiny black door with No. 10 in gold. There was a big cat sitting on the doorstep.

I went up and said "Hello" but the cat said "I'm the Prime Minister's cat and I catch lots of mice, that's my job. I'm very important"

I went to say bye-bye and he smacked
me on the nose with his paw.

That was not a very nice thing to do so I went on my way.
After I crossed over the river I saw one of those
big red buses stop, so I just hopped on.

"That's a good idea," I said to myself.

They started looking at me and talking about me. The bus driver shouted "You haven't got a ticket, I'll get the police" So I jumped off.

I next came across a very tall tower with a large clock on the top.

DING DONG what a noise!

I covered my ears with my paws . They said this was Big Ben,
I couldn't see Ben it just looked like a big tower to me.

The noise was too loud for me so I trotted off on my big adventure.

I looked in wonder at a very large building with black shiny railings and a big black and gold gate which said Buckingham Palace.

There were lots of guards marching up and down.

I saw a very big man with big black shiny boots, a bright red jacket with brass buttons and a big black furry hat. He was standing in front of the black and gold railings and a very big gold gate.

I felt a bit scared of him and didn't want to pass him as his boots looked so big they could squash me.

I then went through the railings and he didn't see me. I can do this because I am just a little puppy.

There were lots of guards marching up and down.

Then two cream coloured dogs with sticky-up ears and little crowns on their heads came running over wagging their tails.

They said," I am Princess Alice and I am called Prince Benjamin.
"We are the Queen's corgis".
I said "I am Fred". "As you are so small we will call you Little Fred."

They said I could play with them but I must only play
on the grass and not go on the flower beds.

We chased each other they took a long time
catching me. I may be only little but I can run very
fast. Their legs are much shorter than mine.

While we were resting as we were hot Prince
Benjamin suddenly sat up and said

" I think that man creeping along over
there is a robber lets go and see",

Prince Benjamin is very clever and knows about these things.

We dashed up and Prince Benjamin told me to
grab his leg, Princess Alice grabbed his arm and
Prince Benjamin grabbed his other leg.

The robber pulled himself free and got away but he left his bag of loot on the grass. We did bark a lot, everyone came to look at the bag and there inside were lots and lots of silver teapots and diamonds.

"I was right" said Prince Benjamin.

The Policemen arrested the robber because we barked so loudly.

A servant called us as he had three bones on a silver platter.
The three of us sat up very nicely as we have been taught.

I wagged my tail as I was so happy, and
he gave each one of us a bone.

"Let Little Fred have the first bone as he is
our guest", said Princess Alice, he has been
a great help in catching the robber.

I couldn't stop wagging my tail as I was so pleased.

Prince Benjamin and Prince Alice stopped chewing their bones because a very nice lady who had on an even bigger crown called them in for their tea.

"That's our mother and she is the Queen". They barked.

She then said "Little Fred you have been such a great help I'm going to give you a silver medal to go round your neck".

I was so happy I gave a big thank you bark.

"Now it's time for you to go home for your tea as your family will be wondering where you are", said the kind lady. Next time I will show you round the Palace.

I quickly said goodbye to Princess Alice and Prince Benjamin and started back home. They asked me to come again and I said yes.

I went through the railings, the guard did not notice me so I went the way I had come.

I arrived home very tired. I went in under the fence. Through the cat flap. Curled up in my nice warm basket and went fast to sleep.

Then I heard them calling me.

"Fred, Fred where are you.

"Oh, there you are, what a good dog"

They said they would give me a nice treat.

I opened both eyes in case I might miss my treat.

I gave my best bark and wagged my tail!

I wish I could tell them about my Big Adventure and my new friends Princess Alice and Prince Benjamin!

Then they looked at me with astonishment
because around my neck was the silver medal

FEARLESS FRED from The Queen